Bonus audiobook available for download at
www.hmhbooks.com/freedownloads.

Password: GALDONE

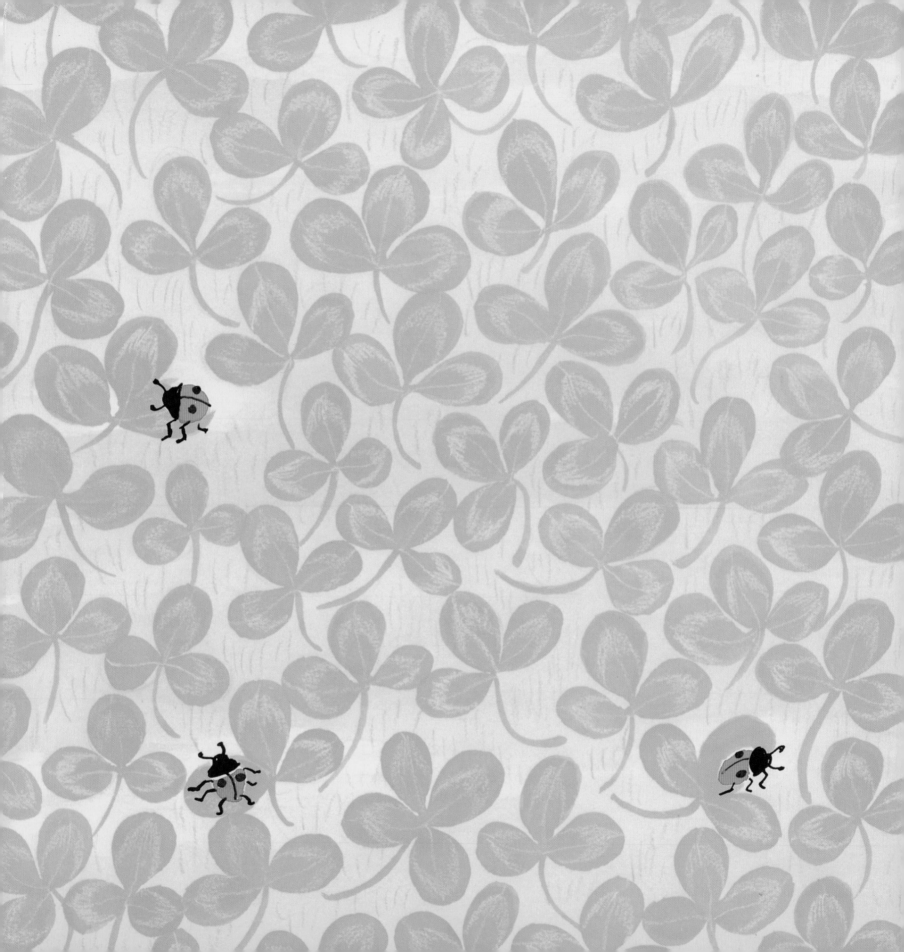

THE FOLK TALE
CLASSICS
TREASURY

Treasury copyright © 2013 by
Houghton Mifflin Harcourt Publishing Company

Published in the United States by HMH Books, an imprint of
Houghton Mifflin Harcourt Publishing Company.

www.hmhbooks.com

ISBN 978-0-544-05247-5

Manufactured in China
SCP 10 9 8 7 6 5 4 3 2 1
4500420768

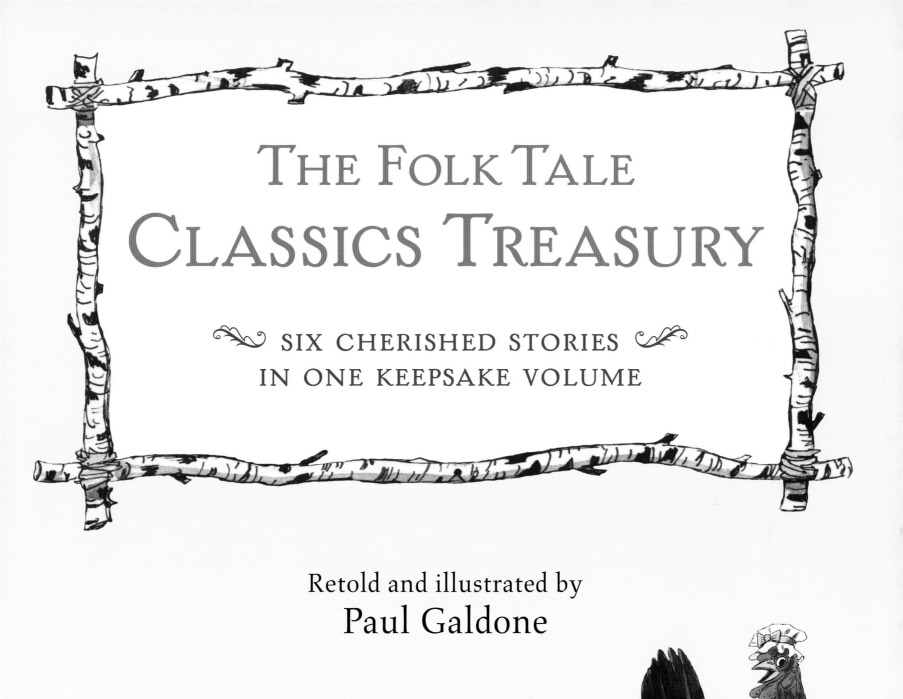

THE FOLK TALE
CLASSICS TREASURY

SIX CHERISHED STORIES
IN ONE KEEPSAKE VOLUME

Retold and illustrated by

Paul Galdone

Houghton Mifflin Harcourt

Boston   New York   2013

CONTENTS

STORY TIME BEGINS WITH "ONCE UPON A TIME..."

What makes a story just right for reading aloud and reading together? The characters should be loveable, the adventures exciting, the situations humorous, and the illustrations lush and colorful. The Folk Tale Classics are all you need for a successful story time! These six stories, lovingly retold and illustrated by Paul Galdone, are timeless tales that have been cherished by children—and grown-ups—for decades. With this treasury, a new generation of readers and storytellers can discover and learn the tales they'll love to tell, hear, and share themselves one day. Story time begins now . . .

The
Little Red Hen

Once upon a time
a cat and a dog and a mouse
and a little red hen
all lived together in a cozy little house.

The cat liked to sleep all day
on the soft couch.

The dog liked to nap all day
on the sunny back porch.

And the mouse liked to snooze all day
in the warm chair by the fireside.

So the little red hen had to do all the housework.

She cooked the meals and washed the dishes
and made the beds. She swept the floor
and washed the windows
and mended the clothes.

She raked the leaves
and mowed the grass
and hoed the garden.

One day when she was hoeing the garden
she found some grains of wheat.

"Who will plant this wheat?"
cried the little red hen.

"Not I," said the cat.

"Not I," said the dog.

"Not I," said the mouse.

"Then I will," said the little red hen. And she did.

Each morning the little red hen watered the wheat and pulled the weeds.

Soon the wheat pushed through the ground and began to grow tall.

When the wheat was ripe,
the little red hen asked,
"Who will cut this wheat?"

"N⬤t I," said the cat.

"N⬤t I," said the dog.

"N⬤t I," said the mouse.

"Then I will," said the little red hen.
And she did.

When the wheat was all cut, the little red hen asked,
"Now, who will take this wheat to the mill
to be ground into flour?"

"Not I," said the cat.

"Not I," said the dog.

"Not I," said the mouse.

"Then I will," said the little red hen. And she did.

The little red hen returned from the mill
carrying a small bag of fine white flour.
"Who will make a cake from this fine white flour?"
asked the little red hen.

"Not I," said the cat.

"Not I," said the dog.

"Not I," said the mouse.

"Then I will," said the little red hen. And she did.

She gathered sticks and made a fire in the stove.
Then she took milk and sugar and eggs and butter
and mixed them in a big bowl
with the fine white flour.

When the oven was hot she poured
the cake batter into a shining pan
and put it in the oven.

Soon a delicious smell
filled the cozy little house.

The cat got off the soft couch
and strolled into the kitchen.

The dog got up from the sunny back porch
and came into the kitchen.

The mouse jumped down from his warm chair
and scampered into the kitchen.

The little red hen
was just taking
a beautiful cake
out of the oven.

"Who will eat this cake?"
asked the little red hen.

"I will!" cried the cat.
"I will!" cried the dog.
"I will!" cried the mouse.

But the little red hen said,

"All by myself
I planted the wheat,
I tended the wheat,
I cut the wheat,
I took the wheat to the mill
to be ground into flour.

All by myself
I gathered the sticks,
I built the fire,
I mixed the cake.
And
all by myself

I am going to eat it!"

And so she did,
to the very last crumb.

After that,

whenever there was work to be done,
the little red hen had three very eager helpers.

The THREE LITTLE PIGS

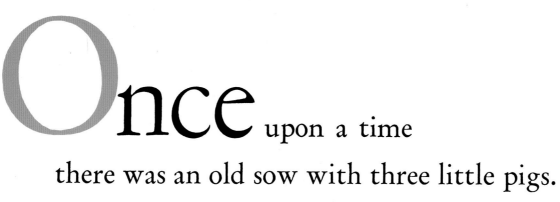

Once upon a time

there was an old sow with three little pigs.

She had no money to keep them,

so she sent them off to seek their fortune.

The first little pig met a man
with a bundle of straw,
and said to him:
"Please, man, give me that straw
to build me a house."

So the man did,
and the little pig
built his house with it.

Along came a wolf.

He knocked at the door, and said:

"Little pig, little pig, let me come in."

"No, no," said the little pig.

"Not by the hair of my chinny chin chin."

"Then I'll huff, and I'll puff,

and I'll blow your house in," said the wolf.

So the wolf huffed, and he puffed,
and he blew the house in.
And he ate up the first little pig.

The second little pig
met a man
with a bundle
of sticks,
and said:
"Please, man,
give me those sticks
to build me a house."

So the man did,
and the little pig built his house with them.

Then along came the wolf, and said:
"Little pig, little pig,
let me come in."

"No, no! Not by the hair
of my chinny chin chin."

"Then I'll huff, and I'll puff,
and I'll blow your house in,"
said the wolf.

So he huffed, and he puffed,
and he huffed and he puffed, and
at last he blew the house in.
And he ate up the second little pig.

The third little pig
met a man
with a load of bricks,
and said:
"Please, man,
give me those bricks
to build me a house."

So the man did,
and the little pig built his house with them.

Soon the same wolf came along,
and said:
"Little pig, little pig,
let me come in."

"No, no! Not by the hair
of my chinny chin chin."

"Then I'll huff, and I'll puff,
and I'll blow your house in,"
said the wolf.

Well, he huffed, and he puffed
and he huffed and he puffed
and he huffed and he puffed.

But he could *not* blow the house in.

At last the wolf stopped
huffing and puffing, and said:
"Little pig, I know where there is
a nice field of turnips."

"Where?" said the little pig.

"On Mr. Smith's farm," said the wolf.
"I will come for you tomorrow morning.
We will go together,
and get some turnips for dinner."

"Very well," said the little pig.
"What time will you come?"

"Oh, at six o'clock," said the wolf.

Well, the little pig got up at five.
He went to Mr. Smith's farm,
and got the turnips
before the wolf came to his house.

"Little pig, are you ready?" asked the wolf.

The little pig said, "Ready!

I have been and come back again

and I got a nice potful of turnips for my dinner."

The wolf was very angry.
But then he thought of another way
to get the little pig, so he said:
"Little pig, I know where
there is a nice apple tree."

"Where?" said the pig.

"Down at Merry Garden," replied the wolf.
"I will come for you
at five o'clock tomorrow morning
and we will get some apples."

Well, the little pig got up
the next morning at four o'clock,
and went off for the apples.
He wanted to get back home before the wolf came.
But it was a long way to Merry Garden,
and then he had to climb the tree.
Just as he was climbing back down
with his basket full of apples,
he saw the wolf coming!

"Little pig!" the wolf said.
"You got here before me!
Are the apples nice?"

"Yes, very," said the little pig.

"I will throw one down to you."

And he threw the apple as far as he could throw.

While the wolf ran to pick it up,

the little pig jumped down and ran home.

The next day the wolf came again
and said to the little pig: "Little pig, there is a fair
at Shanklin this afternoon. Would you like to go?"

"Oh, yes," said the little pig.
"When will you come to get me?"

"At three," said the wolf.

Well, the little pig went off at two o'clock
and bought a butter churn at the fair.

He was going home with it
when he saw the wolf coming!

The little pig jumped into the butter churn to hide.

The churn fell over and rolled
down the hill with the little pig in it.
This frightened the wolf so much
that he turned around and ran home.

Later the wolf went to the little pig's house
and told him what had happened.
"A great round thing came rolling down the hill
right at me," the wolf said.

"Hah, I frightened you then," said the little pig.
"I went to the fair and bought a butter churn.
When I saw you, I got into it,
and rolled down the hill."

The wolf was very angry indeed.
"I'm going to climb down your chimney
and eat you up!" he said.

When the little pig heard the wolf on the roof—

he hung a pot

full of water in the fireplace.

Then he built a blazing fire.

Just as the wolf was coming down the chimney,

the little pig took the cover off the pot,

and in fell the wolf.

The little pig quickly put on the cover again,

boiled up the wolf, and ate him for supper.

And the little pig lived happily ever afterward.

THE THREE BEARS

PAUL GALDONE

nce upon a time there were Three Bears who lived
together in a house of their own in the woods.

one was
a Middle-Sized Bear,

One of them was
a Little Wee Bear,

and the other was
a Great Big Bear.

They each had a bowl for their porridge.

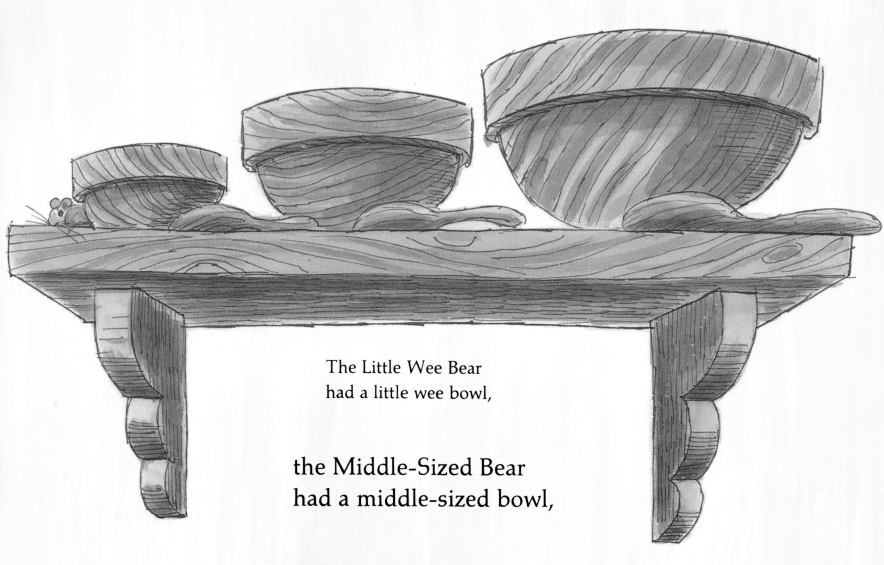

The Little Wee Bear
had a little wee bowl,

the Middle-Sized Bear
had a middle-sized bowl,

and the Great Big Bear
had a great big bowl.

They each had a chair to sit in.

The Little Wee Bear
had a little wee chair,

the Middle-Sized Bear
had a middle-sized chair,

and the Great Big Bear
had a great big chair.

And they each had a bed to sleep in.

The Little Wee Bear
had a little wee bed,

the Middle-Sized Bear
had a middle-sized bed,

and the Great Big Bear
had a great big bed.

One morning, the Three Bears
made porridge for breakfast
and poured it into their bowls.
But it was too hot to eat.
So they decided to go
for a walk in the woods
until it cooled.

While the Three Bears were walking,

a little girl named Goldilocks
came to their house.

First she looked in at the window,

and then she peeked through the keyhole.

Of course there was nobody inside.
Goldilocks turned the handle of the door.

The door was not locked, because
the Three Bears were trusting bears.
They did no one any harm, and never
thought anyone would harm them.

So Goldilocks opened the door and went right in.

There was the porridge
on the table.
It smelled very, very good!

Goldilocks didn't stop to think whose porridge it was.
She went straight to it.

First she tasted the porridge
of the Great Big Bear.
But it was too hot.

Then she tasted the porridge
of the Middle-Sized Bear.
But it was too cold.

Then she tasted the porridge
of the Little Wee Bear.

It was neither too hot nor too cold, but just right. Goldilocks liked it so much that she ate it all up.

Then Goldilocks went into the parlor to see what else she could find.

There were the three chairs.

First she sat down in the chair
of the Great Big Bear.
But it was too hard.

Then she sat down in the chair
of the Middle-Sized Bear.
But it was too soft.

Then she sat down in the chair
of the Little Wee Bear.
It was neither too hard
nor too soft, but just right.
Goldilocks liked it so much
that she rocked and rocked,

until ...

the bottom of the chair fell out!
Down she went—plump!—onto the floor.

Goldilocks went into the bedroom
where the Three Bears slept.

First she lay down upon the bed
of the Great Big Bear.
But it was too high at the head for her.

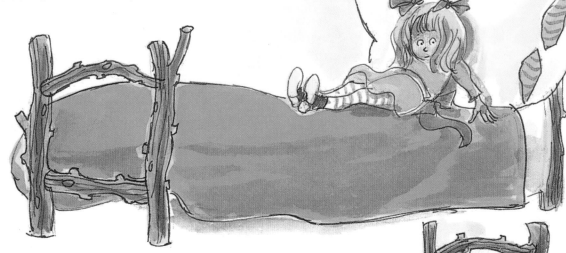

Then she lay down upon the bed
of the Middle-Sized Bear.
But it was too high at the foot for her.

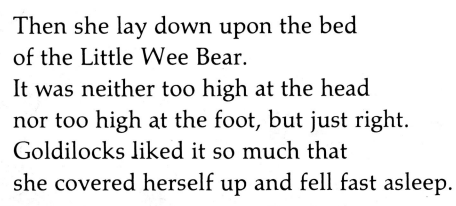

Then she lay down upon the bed
of the Little Wee Bear.
It was neither too high at the head
nor too high at the foot, but just right.
Goldilocks liked it so much that
she covered herself up and fell fast asleep.

By this time,
the Three Bears thought
their porridge
would be cool enough.

So they came home
for breakfast.

113

Goldilocks had left
the spoon of the Great Big Bear
in his porridge bowl.
He noticed it, first thing.

"SOMEBODY HAS BEEN
TASTING MY PORRIDGE!"
said the Great Big Bear
in his great big voice.

Goldilocks had left
the spoon of the Middle-Sized Bear
in her porridge bowl, too.

"SOMEBODY HAS BEEN TASTING MY PORRIDGE!"
said the Middle-Sized Bear
in her middle-sized voice.

Then the Little Wee Bear looked at his bowl.

"SOMEBODY HAS BEEN TASTING MY PORRIDGE
AND HAS EATEN IT ALL UP!"
cried the Little Wee Bear
in his little wee voice.

The Three Bears went
into the parlor.

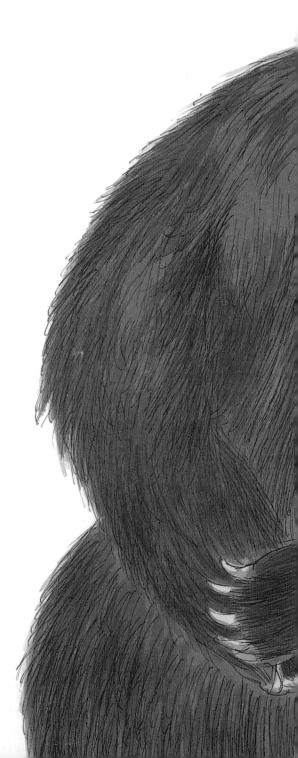

Goldilocks had left
the cushion crooked
in the chair
of the Great Big Bear.
He noticed it, first thing.

"SOMEBODY HAS BEEN
SITTING IN MY CHAIR!"
said the Great Big Bear
in his great big voice.

Goldilocks had squashed down the cushion
in the chair of the Middle-Sized Bear.

"SOMEBODY HAS BEEN SITTING IN MY CHAIR!"
said the Middle-Sized Bear
in her middle-sized voice.

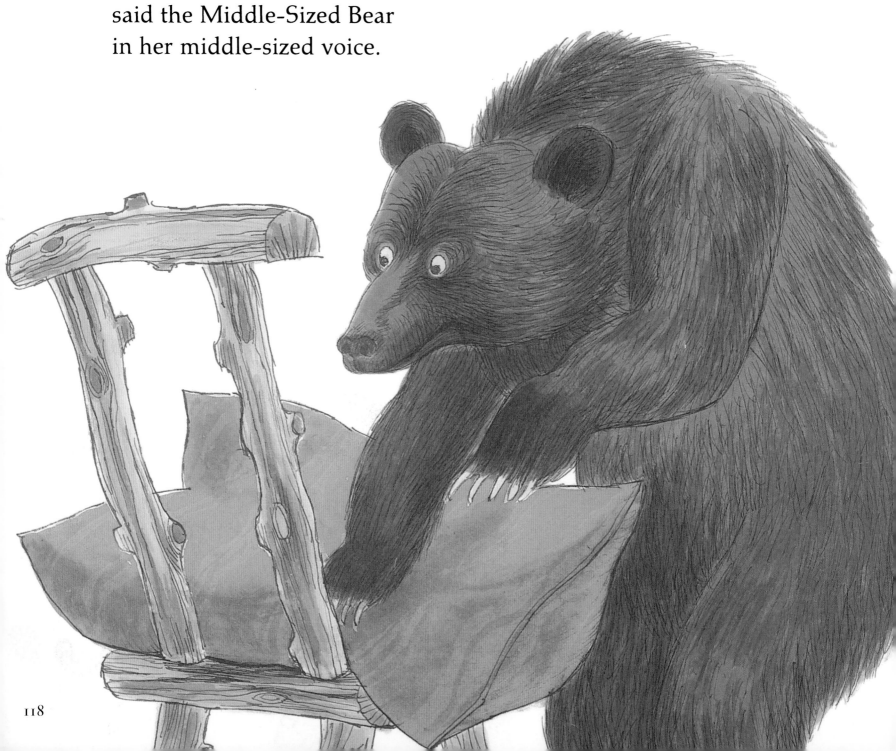

Then the Little Wee Bear looked at his chair.

"SOMEBODY HAS BEEN SITTING IN MY CHAIR
AND HAS SAT RIGHT THROUGH IT!"
cried the Little Wee Bear
in his little wee voice.

The Three Bears went into the bedroom.

Goldilocks had pulled the pillow
of the Great Big Bear out of place.
He noticed it, first thing.

"SOMEBODY HAS BEEN LYING IN MY BED!"
said the Great Big Bear in his great big voice.

120

Goldilocks had pulled the blanket
of the Middle-Sized Bear out of place.

"SOMEBODY HAS BEEN LYING
IN MY BED!"
said the Middle-Sized Bear
in her middle-sized voice.

Then the Little Wee Bear looked at his bed.

"SOMEBODY HAS BEEN LYING IN MY BED—AND HERE SHE IS!"
cried the Little Wee Bear in his little wee voice.

This woke Goldilocks up at once. There were the Three Bears
all staring at her.

Goldilocks was so frightened that
she tumbled out of bed and ran to the open window.

Out she jumped!

And she ran away as fast
as she could, never looking behind her.

No one knows what happened to Goldilocks after that.

As for the Three Bears, they never saw her again.

THE GINGER-BREAD BOY

for Madelon

Once upon a time
there lived a little old woman
and a little old man.
They had no boys or girls
of their own, so they lived
all by themselves
in a little old house.

One day the little old woman
was baking gingerbread.
"I will make a little
Gingerbread Boy," she said.

So she rolled the dough out flat
and cut it in the shape of a little boy.
She made him two good-sized feet.

Then she gave him eyes and a mouth
of raisins and currants,
and stuck on a cinnamon drop for a nose.

She put a row of raisins down the front
of his jacket for buttons.

"There!" she said. "Now we'll have a little Gingerbread Boy of our own."

She put him in the pan, popped him into the oven, and closed the door.

Then she went about her work,
sweeping and cleaning, cleaning and sweeping,
and she forgot all about the little Gingerbread Boy.

Meanwhile he baked brown all over and got very hot.

"Oh my!" said the little old woman
at last, sniffing the air.
"The Gingerbread Boy is burning!"

She ran to the oven and opened the door.
Up jumped the Gingerbread Boy.
He hopped down onto the floor,
ran across the kitchen,
out of the door,
across the garden,
through the gate,
and down the road as fast as
his gingerbread legs could carry him.

The little old woman and the little old man ran after him, shouting:
"Stop! Stop, little Gingerbread Boy!"

The Gingerbread Boy looked back and laughed and called out:

"Run! Run! Run!
Catch me if you can!
You can't catch me!
I'm the Gingerbread Boy,
I am! I am!"

And they couldn't catch him.

So the Gingerbread Boy ran on and on.
Soon he came to a cow.
"Um! um!" sniffed the cow. "You smell good!
Stop, little Gingerbread Boy! I would like to eat you."

But the little Gingerbread Boy laughed and said:

"I've run away from a little old woman,
I've run away from a little old man,
And I can run away from you, I can."

So the cow ran after him. But she couldn't catch him.

The little Gingerbread Boy ran on and on.
Soon he came to a horse.
"Please stop, little Gingerbread Boy,"
said the horse.
"You look very good to eat."

But the little Gingerbread Boy called out:

> "I've run away from a little old woman,
> I've run away from a little old man,
> I've run away from a cow,
> And I can run away from you, I can."

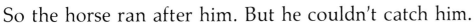

So the horse ran after him. But he couldn't catch him.

By and by the Little Gingerbread Boy came to a barn
where some men were threshing wheat.
The threshers saw the little Gingerbread Boy and called:
"Do not run so fast, little Gingerbread Boy.
Gingerbread boys are made to eat."

But the little Gingerbread Boy ran faster and faster
and shouted:

"I've run away from a little old woman,
  I've run away from a little old man,
  I've run away from a cow,
  I've run away from a horse,
  And I can run away from you,
  I can, I can!"

So the threshers ran after him. But they couldn't catch him.

147

The little Gingerbread Boy ran faster than ever.
Soon he came to a field full of mowers.
When the mowers saw how fine he looked, they called:
"Wait a bit! Wait a bit, little Gingerbread Boy!
Gingerbread boys are made to eat."

But the Gingerbread Boy laughed harder than ever
and ran on like the wind. "Oh, ho! Oh, ho!" he cried:

"I've run away from a little old woman,
I've run away from a little old man,
I've run away from a cow,
I've run away from a horse,
I've run away from a barn full of threshers,
And I can run away from you,
I can, I can!"

149

So the mowers ran after him.

But they couldn't catch him.

By this time the little Gingerbread Boy was very proud
of himself. He strutted, he danced, he pranced!
He thought no one on earth could catch him.

Then he saw a fox coming across the field.
The fox looked at him and began to run.

But the little Gingerbread Boy ran faster still, and shouted:

"Run! Run! Run!
Catch me if you can!
You can't catch me!
I'm the Gingerbread Boy,
I am! I am!
I've run away from a little old woman,
I've run away from a little old man,
I've run away from a cow,
I've run away from a horse,
I've run away from a barn full of threshers,
I've run away from a field full of mowers,
And I can run away from you,
I can! I can!"

"Why," said the fox politely,
"I wouldn't catch you if I could."

Just then the little Gingerbread Boy came to a wide river.
He dared not jump into the water, for he would
crumble to pieces if he did. He looked behind him.
The cow, the horse, and all the people were still
following and getting closer. He had to cross the
river, or they would catch him.

The fox saw this and said,
"Jump on my tail and I will take you across."
So the little Gingerbread Boy jumped onto the fox's tail
and the fox jumped into the river.

When they were out in the river, the fox said:

"Little Gingerbread Boy,
I think you had better get
on my back or you may fall off!"
So the little Gingerbread Boy jumped on the fox's back.

After swimming a little farther, the fox said:

"The water is deep.
You may get wet where you are.
Jump up on my shoulder."

So the little Gingerbread Boy jumped up on the fox's shoulder.

When they were near the
other side of the river,
the fox cried out suddenly:
"The water grows deeper still.
Jump up on my nose!
Jump up on my nose!"

So the little Gingerbread Boy jumped up on the fox's nose.

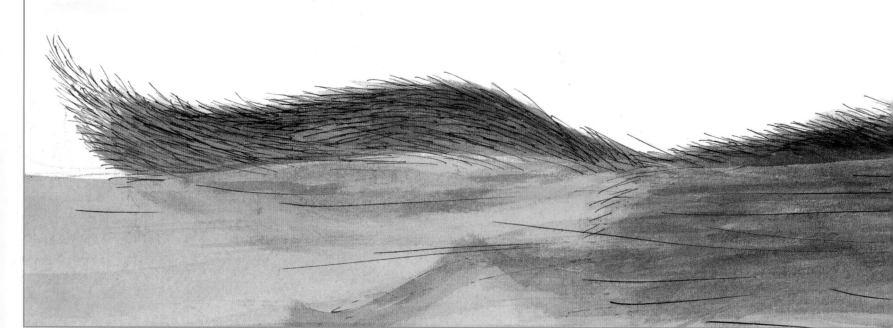

The fox sprang ashore and threw back his head.
Snip—half the Gingerbread Boy was gone.
Snip, Snap—he was three-quarters gone.

Snip, Snap, Snip,
at last and at last
he went the way of
every single gingerbread boy
that ever came
out of an oven....

He was all gone!

So the little old woman and the little old man,
and the cow and the horse,
and the threshers and the mowers,
all went home again...

...while the fox had a good long nap.

Three Little Kittens

For Jamie, Jacob, Nathaniel, and Mariska

Three

Little Kittens

they lost their
mittens,
and they began
to cry,

"Oh, Mother Dear, we sadly fear
Our mittens we have lost!"

"What! lost your mittens,
you naughty kittens!

Then you shall have no pie."

The
three little kittens

found their mittens
and they began to cry,

"Oh! Mother Dear, see here, see here.
Our mittens we have found."

"What!
found your mittens,
you good little kittens,

purrrrr...

purrrr

purr

Then
you shall
have
some pie."
"Purr,
purr,
purr."

The three little kittens

put on their mittens
and soon ate up the pie.

"Oh! Mother Dear, we greatly fear
Our mittens we have soiled."

"What! soiled your mittens,
you naughty kittens!"

Then they
began to sigh,
"Meow,
meow,
meow!"

The three little kittens

washed their mittens,

and hung them up to dry.

"Oh! Mother Dear,
look here, look here,

Our mittens
we have
washed."

"What! washed your mittens,
you darling kittens!

But
hush!
I smell
a rat
close
by."

"Yes, we smell a rat close by.
Meow, meow, *meow!*"

THE THREE BILLY GOATS GRUFF

For Kay

Once upon a time there were three Billy Goats.
They lived in a valley and the name
of all three Billy Goats was "Gruff."

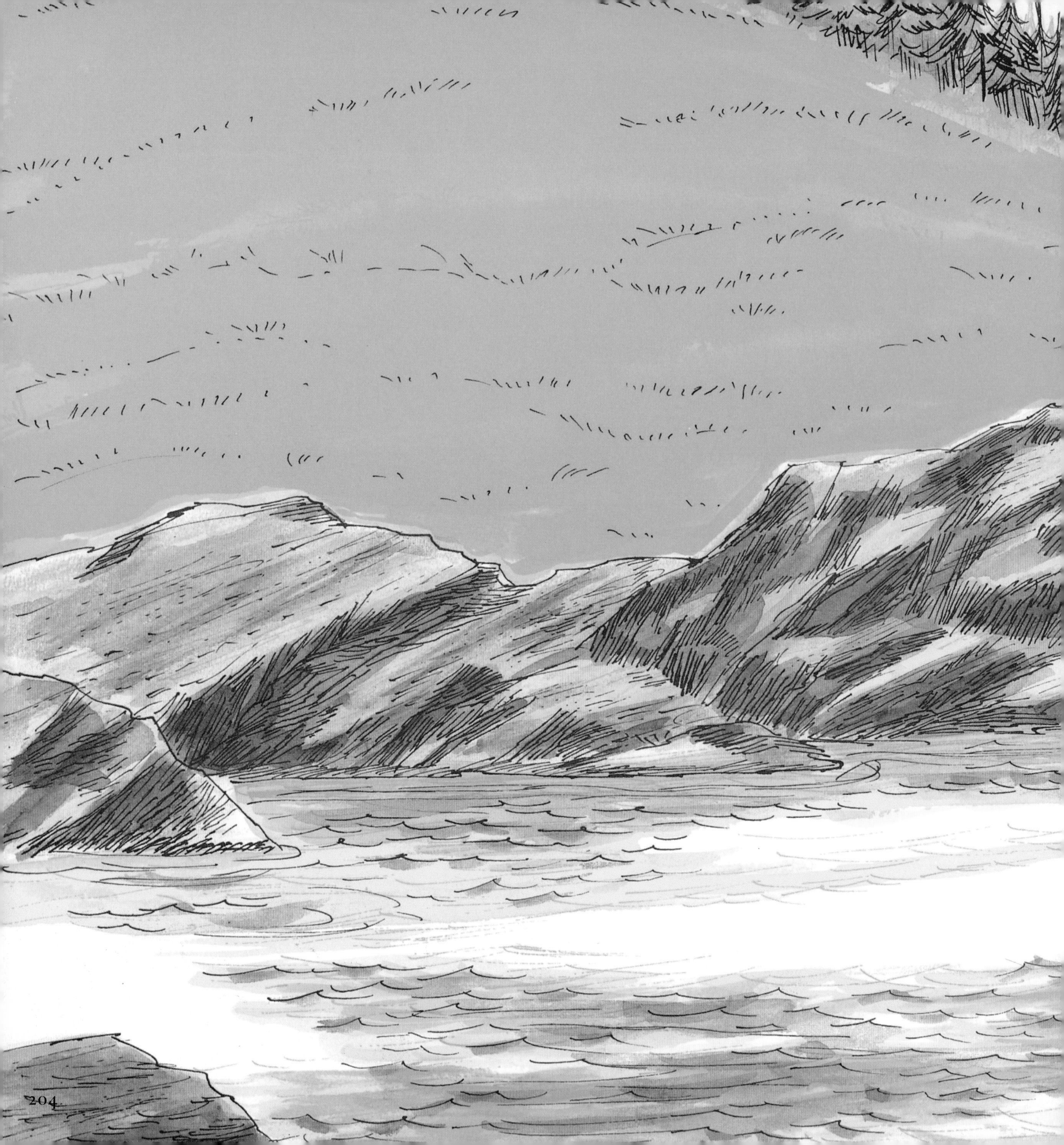

There was very little grass in the valley
and the Billy Goats were hungry.
They wanted to go up the hillside
to a fine meadow full of grass and daisies
where they could eat and eat and eat, and get fat.

But on the way up there was
a bridge over a rushing river.
And under the bridge lived a Troll
who was as mean as he was ugly.

First the youngest Billy Goat Gruff
decided to cross the bridge.

"TRIP, TRAP, TRIP, TRAP!" went the bridge.

"WHO'S THAT TRIPPING OVER MY BRIDGE?"
roared the Troll.

"Oh, it's only I, the tiniest Billy Goat Gruff,"
said the Billy Goat in his very small voice.
"And I'm going to the meadow to make myself fat."

"No you're not," said the Troll,
"for I'm coming to gobble you up!"

"Oh, please don't take me. I'm too little, that I am,"
said the Billy Goat. "Wait till the second
Billy Goat Gruff comes. He's much bigger."

"Well then, be off with you," said the Troll.

211

A little later the second Billy Goat Gruff came to cross the bridge.

"TRIP, TRAP! TRIP, TRAP! TRIP, TRAP!" went the bridge.

"WHO'S THAT TRIPPING OVER MY BRIDGE?" roared the Troll.

"Oh, it's only I, the second Billy Goat Gruff,
and I'm going up to the meadow to make myself fat,
said the Billy Goat.
And his voice was not so small.

"No you're not," said the Troll,
"for I'm coming to gobble you up!"

"Oh, please don't take me. Wait a little, till the
third Billy Goat Gruff comes. He's much bigger."

"Very well, be off with you," said the Troll.

Then up came the third Billy Goat Gruff.

"TRIP, TRAP! TRIP, TRAP!
TRIP, TRAP! TRIP, TRAP!"
went the bridge.

The third Billy Goat Gruff was so heavy
that the bridge creaked and groaned under him.

"WHO'S THAT TRAMPING OVER MY BRIDGE?"
roared the Troll.

"IT IS I, THE BIG BILLY GOAT GRUFF,"
said the Billy Goat.
And his voice was as loud as the Troll's.

"Now I'm coming to gobble you up!" roared the Troll.

"Well, come along!" said the big Billy Goat Gruff.
"I've got two horns and four hard hooves.
See what you can do!"

So up climbed that mean, ugly Troll,
and the big Billy Goat Gruff butted him with his horns,
and he trampled him with his hard hooves,

and he tossed him over the bridge
into the rushing river.

Then the big Billy Goat Gruff went up the hillside to join his brothers.

229

In the meadow
the three Billy Goats Gruff
got so fat that they could hardly
walk home again.
They are probably there yet.

So snip, snap, snout,
This tale's told out.

The Folk Tale Classics are stories that were lovingly and wittily retold and illustrated by Paul Galdone. Mr. Galdone was born in Budapest in 1907 and lived in New York's Hudson Valley and Vermont, where he was inspired to create the pastoral and woodland settings in his books. For decades, his work has been cherished for its humor and, above all, for its appeal to children. Winner of a Caldecott Honor award, he illustrated more than three hundred books in his lifetime, many of which are classic retellings like the ones collected here.

PHOTO BY JOANNA GALDONE

Discover and share all of the Folk Tale Classics!

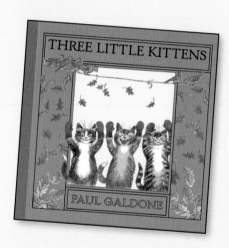

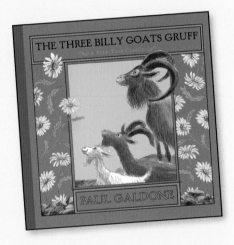

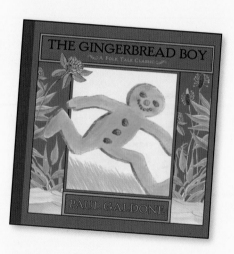

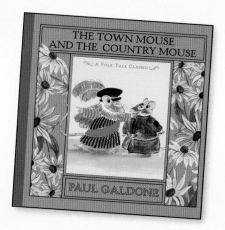

THE TOWN MOUSE
AND THE COUNTRY MOUSE

PAUL GALDONE

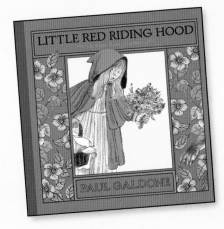

LITTLE RED RIDING HOOD

PAUL GALDONE

HENNY PENNY
A FOLK TALE CLASSIC

PAUL GALDONE

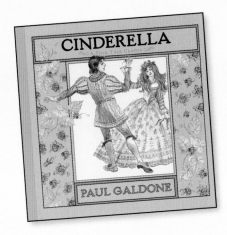

CINDERELLA
A FOLK TALE CLASSIC

PAUL GALDONE

THE FOLK TALE CLASSICS
HEIRLOOM LIBRARY

PAUL GALDONE

THE FOLK TALE CLASSICS
KEEPSAKE COLLECTION

PAUL GALDONE

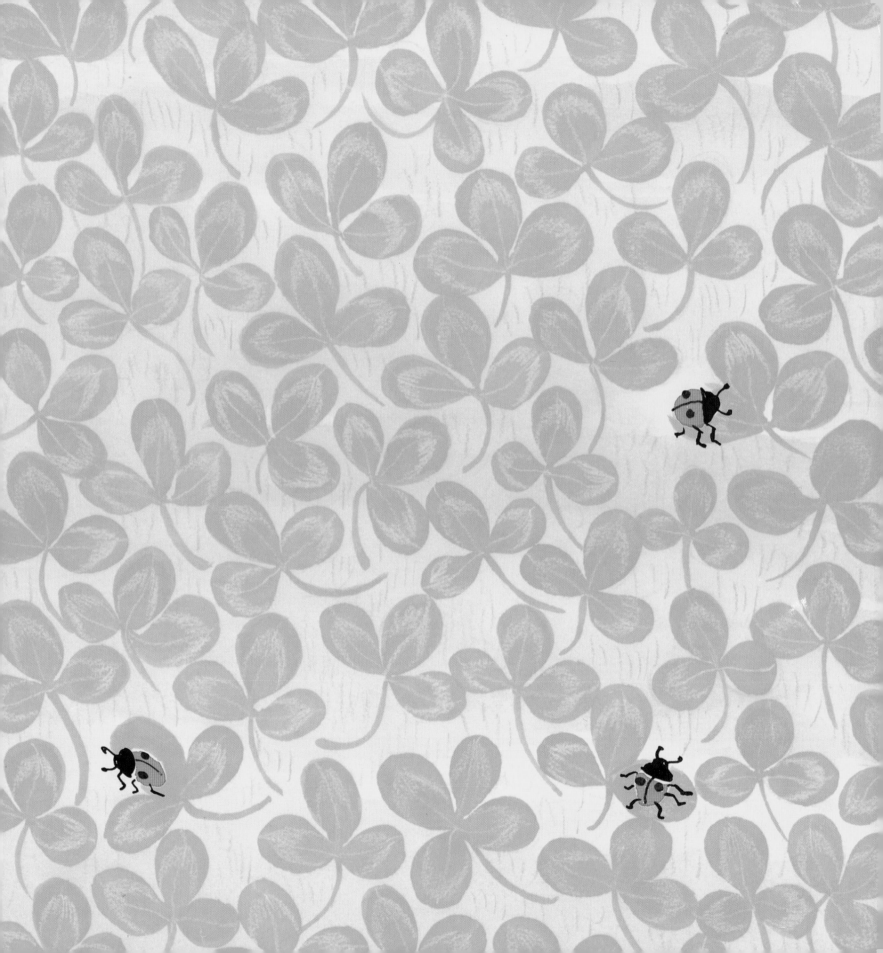

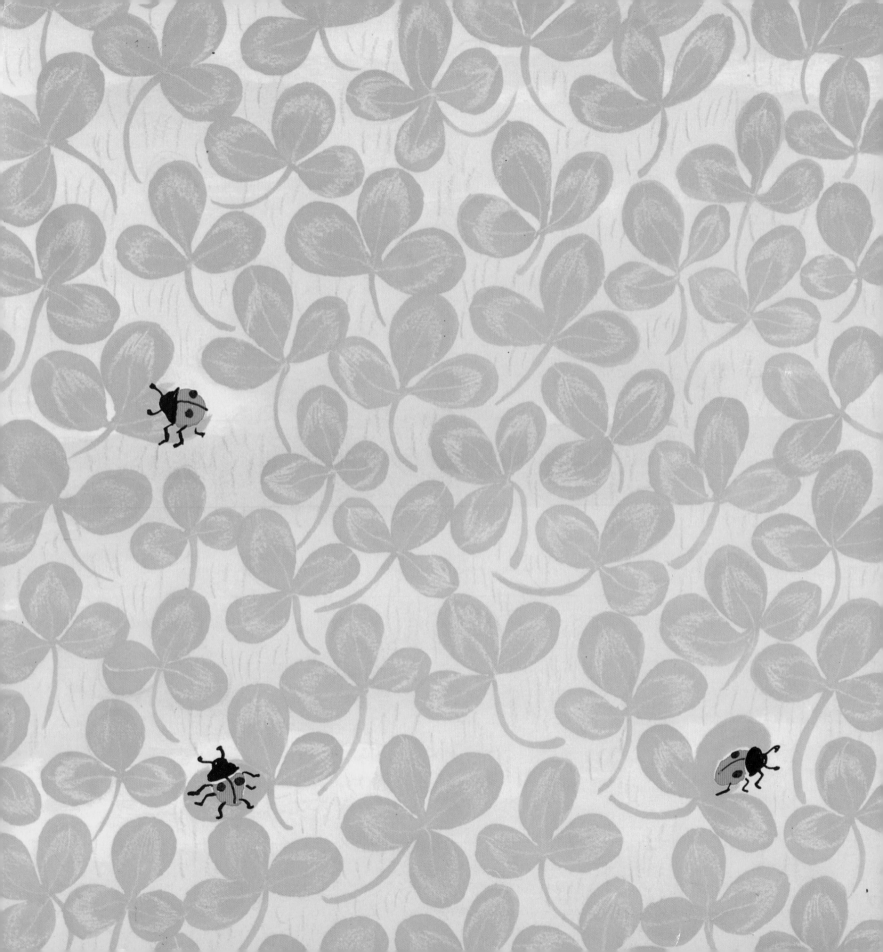